D0014459

This Ladybird Book belongs to:

_____

_____

_____

_____

*This Ladybird retelling*
*by*
*Nicola Baxter*

Ladybird books are widely available, but in case of
difficulty may be ordered by post or telephone from:

Ladybird Books – Cash Sales Department
Littlegate Road  Paignton  Devon TQ3 3BE
Telephone 0803 554761

A catalogue record for this book is available
from the British Library

Published by Ladybird Books Ltd  Loughborough  Leicestershire  UK
Ladybird Books Inc  Auburn  Maine 04210  USA

© LADYBIRD BOOKS LTD 1993
LADYBIRD and the device of a Ladybird are trademarks of Ladybird Books Ltd
*All rights reserved. No part of this publication may be reproduced,*
*stored in a retrieval system, or transmitted in any form or by any*
*means, electronic, mechanical, photocopying, recording or otherwise,*
*without the prior consent of the copyright owner.*

# Puss
# in Boots

*illustrated*
*by*
*TONY KENYON*

*based on the story by Charles Perrault*

Once upon a time there was a miller who had three sons. When the miller died, he left the mill to his eldest son and a donkey to his second son. They were able to set to work straightaway.

But all that was left for the youngest son was his father's cat.

"Poor Puss," said the miller's son. "How shall we manage?"

"Don't worry," said the cat. "Give me a pair of boots and a bag and we will do very well together."

When the miller's son brought the things the cat wanted, Puss got ready. He put on his boots and left the bag, filled with lettuce leaves, in a field.

Very soon, a little rabbit came to nibble the lettuce.

Quick as a flash, Puss caught the
rabbit in his bag and carried it to the
King's palace.

"Your Majesty," said Puss, "please
accept this fine rabbit as a present
from my master, the Marquis of
Carrabas."

"I've never heard of him," said the
King, "but you deserve a treat from
the kitchen."

The next day, Puss heard that the King and his daughter would be driving by the river.

"Master," he said, "do what I say and we shall be rich. You must take off your clothes and swim in the river. And you must believe that your name is the Marquis of Carrabas."

"I've never heard of him," said the miller's son, "but I'll do as you say, Puss."

Before long, the King drove past with his daughter, the Princess. He was pleased to see Puss again.

"Your Majesty," said Puss, bowing low, "a very terrible thing has happened. My master, the Marquis of Carrabas, was swimming in the river when some thieves came and stole all his clothes!"

"How dreadful!" exclaimed the King and the Princess together.

The King sent off to the palace at once for some clothes. When the miller's son put them on, he looked very handsome.

"Please come and ride in our carriage," said the King. "May I present my daughter?"

Puss ran quickly on ahead. When he saw some men making hay in a field, he shouted to them, "The King is coming. If he asks, you must say that this land belongs to the Marquis of Carrabas."

"We've never heard of him," said the
haymakers, "but we'll do as you say."

Soon the King drove past in his carriage with the Princess and the miller's son. "Tell me, my man," said the King to a haymaker, "whose land is this?"

"It belongs to the Marquis of Carrabas, Your Majesty," the man replied at once.

Meanwhile, Puss had found out that the land was really owned by an ogre who lived in a huge castle nearby.

Puss quickly made his way to the castle and knocked on the door. "Sir, is it true that you are a very good magician?" he asked the ogre.

The ogre, who liked to show off, replied, "Yes, it's true. I can even turn myself into a lion!"

Quick as a flash, the ogre became a fierce, roaring lion!

Puss was so startled that he scrambled
to the top of a chest of drawers to
hide.

When the ogre had changed himself
back again, Puss jumped down.
"Turning into a lion must be easy for
someone as big and strong as you," he
said. "But can you turn yourself into
something *tiny* – like a mouse?"

"Of course I can!" roared the ogre.
"Just watch!"

In the blink of an eye, the ogre became a little mouse scurrying across the floor. Puss instantly pounced on him and ate him up.

"Now that the ogre is gone," Puss said to himself, "this castle will make a very fine home for my master, the Marquis of Carrabas."

The King was most impressed by the handsome young man who owned such rich land and lived in such a magnificent castle. "He would make a fine husband for my daughter," the King said.

So the miller's son and the Princess and Puss lived happily ever after. And now *everyone* has heard of the Marquis of Carrabas!